For Tien and Reid

BEACH LANE BOOKS
An imprint of Simon & Schuster Children's Publishing Division
1230 Avenue of the Americas, New York, New York 10020

Book design by Lauren Rille
The text for this book is set in Calvert.
The illustrations for this book are rendered digitally.
Manufactured in China
1013 SCP
First Edition
10 9 8 7 6 5 4 3 2 1
Library of Congress Cataloging-in-Publication Data
Austin, Mike, 1963–
Junkyard / Mike Austin.—1st ed.
p. cm.
Summary: Munching Machines enter a huge junkyard and consume all of the waste, then smooth the ground, plant trees and flowers, create a lake and playground, and much more.
ISBN 978-1-4424-5961-8 (hardcover)
ISBN 978-1-4424-5962-5 (eBook)
[1. Reclamation of land—Fiction. 2. Junk—Fiction. 3. Robots—Fiction.] I. Title.
PZ8.3.A93722Jun 2013
[E]—dc23
2012042199

JUNKYARD

Mike Austin

Beach Lane Books
New York London Toronto Sydney New Delhi

ABC

A yard full of junk!
Piles of junk!
Junk as far as the eye can see—
not even room for one little tree.

It's time to clean up,
to make something new.
The Munching Machines
know just what to do!

They munch rusty school buses,
cars, and old planes,
tugboats and sailboats
and anchors and chains.

They chew broken bed frames,
worn-out rubber tires,
leaky bathtubs, smelly toilets,
and miles of tangled wires!

They crunch boxcars, jelly jars,
crooked airplane wings.
And five dirty dump trucks
filled with curly metal springs.

Jelly
CORN
ONIONS
PEAS
CARROTS

They chomp messy mounds of shopping carts,
picture frames, and bicycles,
broken chairs, table lamps,
and squeaking rusty tricycles.

They slurp truckloads of stinky fish oil,
barrels of sticky paste,
a swimming pool of goopy goo,
and tubs of toxic waste!

BURP!
OIL

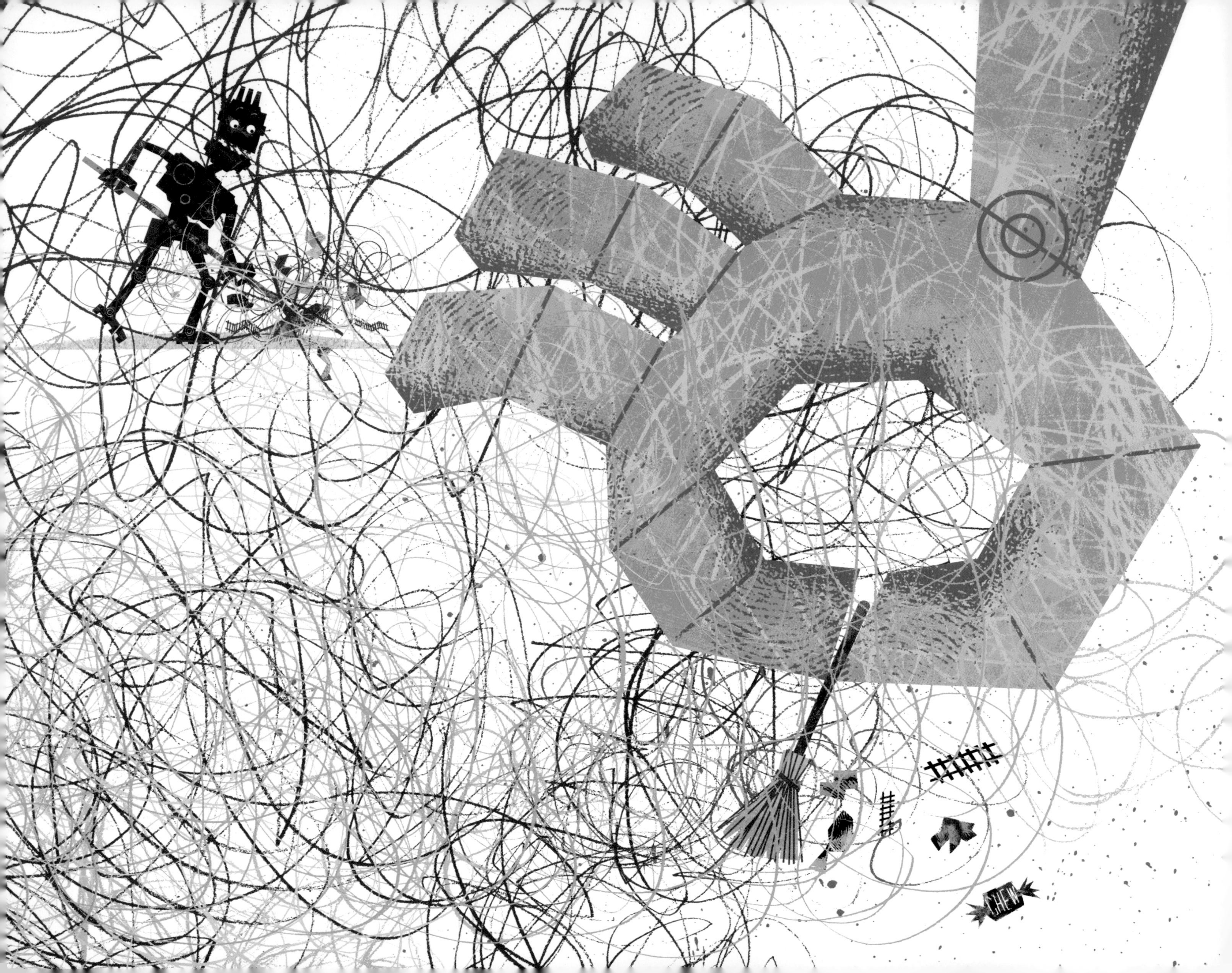
CHEW

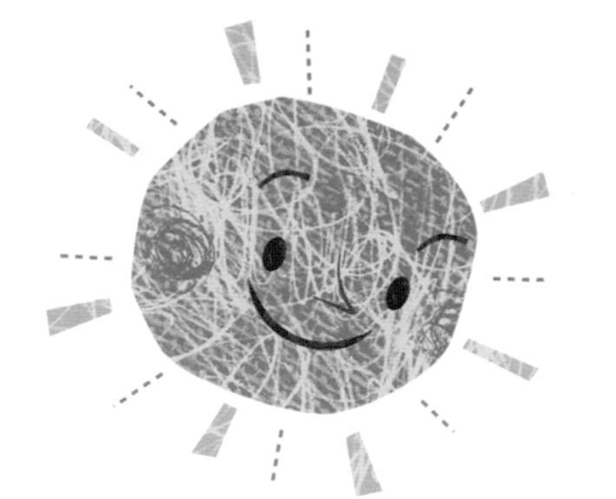

Then they sweep the yard clean
from the front to the back
until all that remains is one little stack
of bubble gum wrappers and a toy train track!

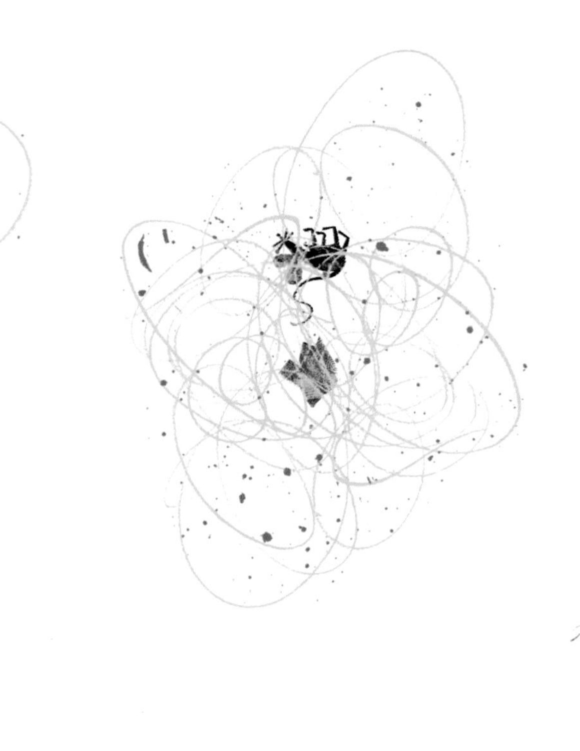

Hooray!

All clean!

It's time for something new!

The Munching Machines know just what to do.

They dig hundreds of holes
for hundreds of trees,
and sow hundreds of flowers
for hungry honeybees!

Hello, honey!

SILO
Hungry! Hungry! Hungry!

They build a playground full of slippy slides,
tire swings, and tree forts,
a sandy beach for volleyball,
a soccer field, and tennis courts!

They dig a lake for splashing
and swimming and boating,
and a meandering river
for fishing and floating!

They pile dirt high
to make mountains for hiking
and a long winding trail
for running and biking.

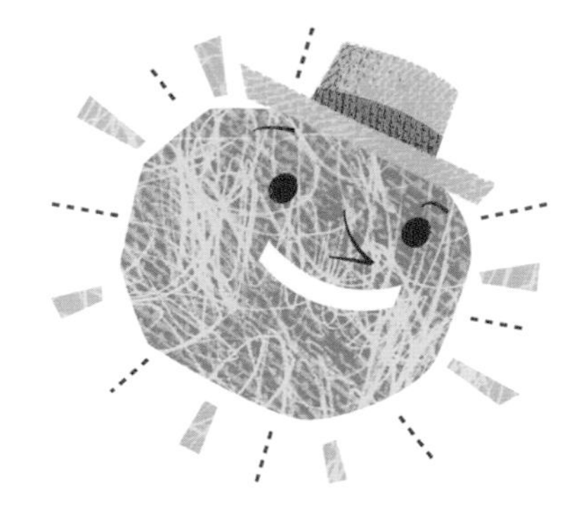

They plant a big garden
full of corn and tomatoes,
broccoli, carrots,
peas, and potatoes!

They blow up balloons
and mail invitations.
"Almost done!" they say.

Hooray!

Only one thing left to do.
Ready? Get set . . .

FUN!
ALL WELCOME!
CELEBRATE!
COME ONE! COME ALL!

LOVE

PLAY!
AIR MAIL
TO: HAWAII